KINGFISHER

Larousse Kingfisher Chambers Inc.
95 Madison Avenue
New York, New York 10016

First American edition 1995
2 4 6 8 10 9 7 5 3 1

LIBRARY OF CONGRESS CATALOGING-IN-PUBLICATION DATA
Lévy, Didier.
[Albert le craneur. English]
Albert / written by Didier Lévy; illustrated by Coralie
Gallibour—1st American ed.
p. cm.
Summary: Albert the pig imagines himself the finest in the
pigsty and expects to become a movie star, admired by pretty lady
pigs in bikinis and envied by gentlemen pigs.
[1. Pigs–Fiction. 2. Pride and vanity–Fiction.] I. Gallibour,
Coralie, ill. II. Title
PZ7.L5826A1 1995
[E]–dc20 94-48721 CIP AC

ISBN 1-85697-621-1

ALBERT

A STORY BY
DIDIER LÉVY

ENGLISH TEXT BY
ANTHEA BELL

ILLUSTRATED BY
CORALIE GALLIBOUR

Kingfisher
NEW YORK

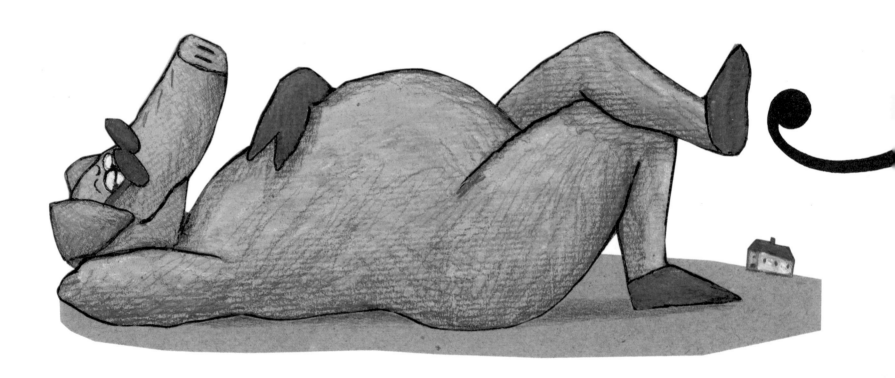

Albert was a show-off.
In the pigsty he was interested
in no one but himself.

Albert was the most beautiful!
Albert was the fattest!
Albert was the pinkest!
Albert had the nicest
corkscrew tail of all!

From morning to night he strutted
around, totally pleased with his
own perfection.

Not only was Albert a show-off,
he also had a wicked sense of humor.

One afternoon, when the other pigs lay
down for a nap, Albert read them recipes
for Pork Chops with Mushrooms, or

Ham with Madeira Sauce.

It wasn't long before he had the other
pigs crying and begging him to stop.
Albert just smoked his cigar and dreamed
of Hollywood and lady pigs in bikinis.

Handsome, strong, and intelligent as he was,
Albert was sure he would become a movie star.
All the lady pigs would be crazy about him.
All the gentlemen pigs would want to be like him.
He would be known as Albert the Magnificent,
idol of every pigsty and farmyard!

With such class and such elegance, Albert would be offered all the great roles: cowboy heroes, daring spies, good-hearted outlaws! He would even play Superpig, taking revenge on all the world's butchers, the enemies of pigs, by turning them into fat garlic sausages.

Once famous, Albert would be able to do anything he liked. If he liked, he would have twenty pounds of strawberry jam at every meal. And he would have those twenty pounds of strawberry jam brought to him by three pretty lady pigs in bikinis.

Albert dreamed on. If he wanted, he would even marry Pigetta Wilson, the great movie star—the divine Pigetta, who was every pig's dream. He would eat strawberry jam while she told him how wonderful he was.

That would be the life!

While he dreamed of Hollywood, strawberry jam, and Pigetta Wilson, Albert was not aware of anything else. He didn't watch where he was walking, for example. And then what happened? A banana skin got in his way!

Covered in filth and smelling foul, Albert wasn't so proud. This time the other pigs got a good laugh. They read him the recipe for Show-off with Garbage Sauce, an excellent recipe that all the pigs were crazy about.

Except Albert, of course.

CORALIE GALLIBOUR

is an artist who is very popular with pigs.

If you ever happen to be in the part of Paris

where she lives, you may meet a pig dressed to kill.

Follow that pig: you can bet it's on its way to

Coralie's studio to have its portrait painted!

DIDIER LÉVY

has always been extremely fond of pigs and

very close to them. His mother says this is not

surprising, considering what a pig he is himself

and seeing as his room has always been

a pigsty. So he is just the person to tell us the

wonderful tale of Albert.